BEAR IS A BEAR

WRITTEN BY
JONATHAN STUTZMAN

ILLUSTRATED BY
DAN SANTAT

BALZER + BRAY
An Imprint of HarperCollins Publishers

Balzer + Bray is an imprint of HarperCollins Publishers.

Bear Is a Bear
Text copyright © 2021 by Jonathan Stutzman
Illustrations copyright © 2021 by Dan Santat
All rights reserved. Manufactured in Italy.
Library of Congress Control Number: 2020948229
ISBN 978-0-06-288051-2

The artist used watercolor, pencil, and Adobe Photoshop to create the illustrations. No bears
(real or stuffed) were harmed in the making of this book.
Hand-lettering by Dan Santat
Typography by Dana Fritts
21 22 23 24 25   RTLO   10 9 8 7 6 5 4 3 2 1
❖
First Edition

For my mom,
who is full of love
—J.S.

For Leah
—D.S.

Bear is a bear hopeful and shy.

Bear is a bear full of love.

Bear is a new friend.

Bear is a snack.

Bear is a tissue.

Bear is a soft, warm pillow.

Bear is a bear covered in fuzz.

Bear is a bear full of love.

Bear is a fancy lady.

Bear is a pirate.

Bear is a ghost.

Bear is a brave protector.

Bear is a bear steadfast and snug.

Bear is a bear full of love.

Bear is a bold explorer.

Bear is a bookworm.

Bear is an artist.

Bear is a bear covered in chalk.
Bear is a bear full of love.

Bear is a scientist.

Bear is a dreamer.

Bear is a tissue.

Bear is a soft, warm pillow.

Bear is a bear aging and worn.

Bear is a bear full of love.

Bear is a piece of home.

Bear is a scholar.

Bear is a distraction.

Bear is a memory.

Bear is a bear covered in dust.

Bear is a bear full of love.

Bear is remembered.

Bear is an old friend.

Bear is a new friend.

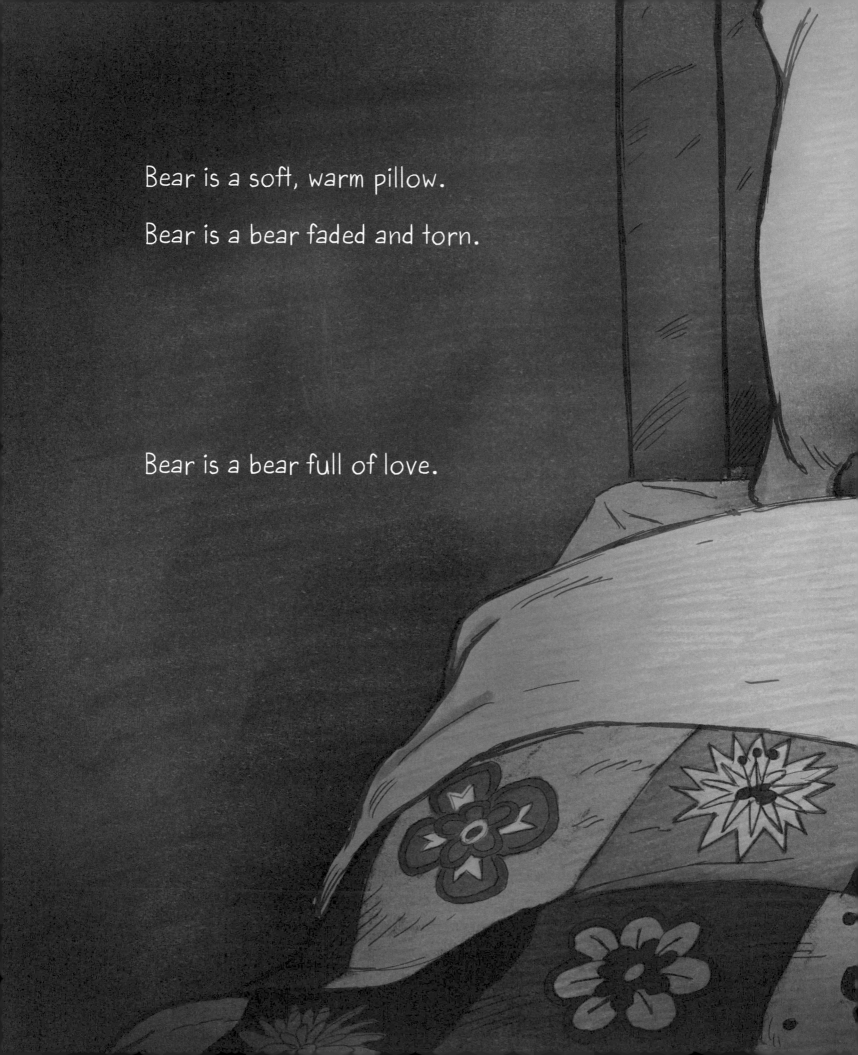

Bear is a soft, warm pillow.

Bear is a bear faded and torn.

Bear is a bear full of love.